For Maria Modugno

A Pet for Petunia
Copyright © 2011 by Paul Schmid
All rights reserved. Manufactured in China.
No part of this book may be used or reproduced in any manner whatsoever without written permission except in the case of brief
quotations embodied in critical articles and reviews. For information address HarperCollins Children's Books,
a division of HarperCollins Publishers, 10 East 53rd Street, New York, NY 10022. www.harpercollinschildrens.com

Library of Congress Cataloging-in-Publication Data
Schmid, Paul.
    A pet for Petunia / Paul Schmid. — 1st ed.
        p. cm.
    Summary: Petunia so desperately wants a pet skunk that she refuses to believe her parents when they say skunks stink.
    ISBN 978-0-06-196331-5 (trade bdg.)
    ISBN 978-0-06-196332-2 (lib. bdg.)
    [1. Skunks—Fiction. 2. Parent and child—Fiction. 3. Humorous stories.] I. Title.
PZ7.S3492 Pet 2011   2009039667
[E]—dc22   CIP
                                                              AC

Typography by Dana Fritts 11 12 13 14 15 SCP 10 9 8 7 6 5 4 3 2 1 ❖ First Edition

4728

a pet for Petunia

paul schmid

HARPER

An Imprint of HarperCollinsPublishers

Petunia likes skunks.
No, that's not exactly right.

Petunia **LOVES** skunks!

"They have cute little noses.
They have big black eyes.

They're black and white
and they have STRIPES!"

Petunia tells anyone who will listen
just how perfectly awesome skunks are.

Petunia *wants, wants, wants!* a REAL pet skunk.

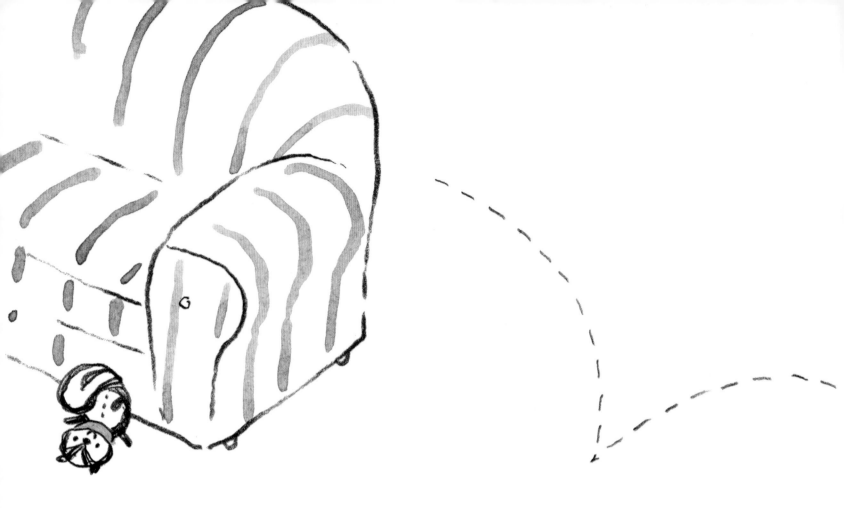

"Please, please, please!
May I have a pet skunk?
Pleeeease?" she begs her parents.

"But, but, but . . . ," begin her parents.
But Petunia isn't listening.
"I'll feed my skunk every day.
I promise! Really!" says Petunia.

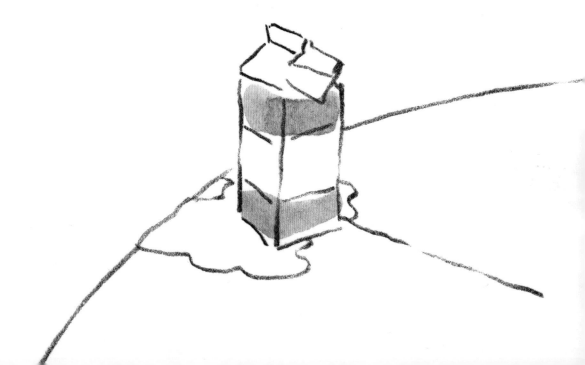

"I'll take her for walks!"

"I'll read stories to Skunkie.
And draw her pictures!
You'll see!" says Petunia.

Petunia assures her parents
she will clean the skunk's
litter box too.

"Every week. Day! Hour!
Whatever! Promise!

Please, please, please
may I have a pet skunk?
Please!"

"What!
Why not?"

"They stink," say her parents.

"STINK?

How can you say that!

They don't STINK! They're CUTE!

Of all the . . . **This is so not fair!**

I'll tell you what stinks! THIS stinks!

You just don't love me. *THAT'S what it is.*

They do NOT stink! Stink, my foot! You wanna

see stink? I'll show you stink! You don't know how much

I love skunks. **I *need* a pet skunk. I'll *die*** if I don't have a pet skunk!

You said no when I wanted a python, too! I bet Katie's parents would get

HER a skunk. *Why did I have to get born into THIS family?* I bet skunks smell ***great!***

Well, I'm not giving up! A girl's gotta do what a girl's gotta do. . . ."

With such disappointing lunkheads for parents,
naturally Petunia *must* leave home.

"I'll live in the woods," thinks Petunia.
"I'll get eaten by a bear. *Then* they'll
let me have my pet skunk!"

Petunia follows a path to some trees.

And there.

On the path.

Is a skunk.

Black and white.
Cute little nose.
Big black eyes.
Stripes.

Petunia stares at the skunk.

The skunk stares at Petunia.

Petunia gives a joyful gasp.

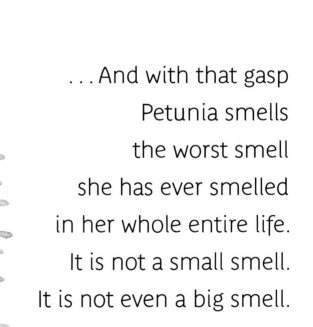

. . . And with that gasp
Petunia smells
the worst smell
she has ever smelled
in her whole entire life.
It is not a small smell.
It is not even a big smell.

It is a STINK!

An *awful* stink!

A *horrible* stink!

A *humongous* stink!

Tears flood Petunia's eyes.
A lump bulges in her throat.

Petunia turns.
She runs.
Runs back home.
Runs to her room.
Into her bed.

It is a while before Petunia
can speak.

"Skunks . . . are . . . so . . .
AWESOME!" she whoops.

Petunia giggles and adds:
"*Awesomely* **STINKY**!"

Then, gazing at
big black eyes,
a cute little nose, and
stripes, stripes, stripes,
Petunia decides she
already has a
perfectly
awesome pet.

Until . . .

she sees that absolutely, totally,
major sweet porcupine!